A Note to Parents and Caregivers:

Read-it! Readers are for children who are just starting on the amazing road to reading. These beautiful books support both the acquisition of reading skills and the love of books.

 The PURPLE LEVEL presents basic topics and objects using high frequency words and simple language patterns.

 The RED LEVEL presents familiar topics using common words and repeating sentence patterns.

 The BLUE LEVEL presents new ideas using a larger vocabulary and varied sentence structure.

 The YELLOW LEVEL presents more challenging ideas, a broad vocabulary, and wide variety in sentence structure.

 The GREEN LEVEL presents more complex ideas, an extended vocabulary range, and expanded language structures.

 The ORANGE LEVEL presents a wide range of ideas and concepts using challenging vocabulary and complex language structures.

When sharing a book with your child, read in short stretches, pausing often to talk about the pictures. Have your child turn the pages and point to the pictures and familiar words. And be sure to reread favorite stories or parts of stories.

There is no right or wrong way to share books with children. Find time to read with your child, and pass on the legacy of literacy.

Adria F. Klein, Ph.D.
Professor Emeritus
California State University
San Bernardino, California

Editor: Christianne Jones
Page Production: Tracy Kaehler
Creative Director: Keith Griffin
Editorial Director: Carol Jones

First American edition published in 2006 by
Picture Window Books
5115 Excelsior Boulevard
Suite 232
Minneapolis, MN 55416
877-845-8392
www.picturewindowbooks.com

First published in 2005 by
Allegra Publishing Limited
Unit 13/15 Quayside Lodge
William Morris Way
Townmead Road
London SW6 2UZ UK

Printed in the United States of America.

Library of Congress Cataloging-in-Publication Data
Law, Felicia.
Rumble meets Lucas Lizard / by Felicia Law ; illustrated by Yoon-Mi Pak.
p. cm. — (Read-it! readers)
Summary: Rumble's Cave Hotel is open but there are no guests, so Rumble allows
a designer to give the place a makeover, all the while worrying that he will not like
the results.
ISBN 1-4048-1334-9 (hard cover)
[1. Interior decoration—Fiction. 2. Hotels, motels, etc.—Fiction. 3. Lizards—
Fiction. 4. Dragons—Fiction. 5. Spiders—Fiction.] I. Pak, Yoon Mi, ill. II. Title.
III. Series.

PZ7.L41835Ruml 2005
[E]—dc22   2005027180

Rumble Meets Lucas Lizard

by Felicia Law
illustrated by Yoon-Mi Pak

Special thanks to our advisers for their expertise:

Adria F. Klein, Ph.D.
Professor Emeritus, California State University
San Bernardino, California

Susan Kesselring, M.A.
Literacy Educator
Rosemount–Apple Valley–Eagan (Minnesota) School District

PICTURE WINDOW BOOKS
Minneapolis, Minnesota

This is the life of a cool, young dragon named Rumble. When his grandma leaves her run-down cave to him, Rumble sets about making it into a four-star hotel. He doesn't do it all alone. He has help from a picky hotel inspector and an annoying spider named Shelby.

Rumble has opened his new hotel, but he doesn't have any guests. Rumble needs a designer to make the hotel look and feel more like home, and that's when Lucas Lizard shows up. He is ready to make things beautiful. But will Rumble like how Lucas decorates his hotel?

Rumble's Cave Hotel was open. Rumble had painted the hotel's sign himself.

"Now we wait," he said.

"For what?" asked Shelby Spider.

"Guests!" said Rumble. "Lots and lots of guests."

The days passed, but no guests arrived.
Then Buddy Beaver came. He wanted a bed
for the night. But there were no beds.

"This is a funny hotel," said Buddy Beaver.
"It doesn't have any beds."

"It's simple," said Shelby Spider. "Simple
is OK."

"You're lucky I'm a carpenter," said Buddy.
"I'll build some beds."

And he did just that. Rumble had Buddy
Beaver build beds for every room in
his hotel.

But even with beds there were no guests.

"Maybe this hotel is TOO simple,"
said Rumble.

"No way!" said Shelby Spider. "Simple
is OK."

"But there are no rugs on the floor, no
curtains on the windows, and no pictures on
the walls," said Rumble.

"Pictures gather dust, and you don't like
dust," said Shelby. "You said 'NO' to my
cobwebs and now you want curtains?"

"But it doesn't feel like home," said Rumble.

11

"I agree," said a voice from the doorway. "Lucas Lizard at your service, Mr. Rumble," he said with a deep bow. "I'm a master of design and a king of style. I can see your hotel has neither—no design and no style."

"I told you we needed help," Rumble said to Shelby.

"It's simple," said Shelby Spider. "And simple is OK."

"Hmm!" said Lucas Lizard, looking at the bare walls and bare floor.

"To design is to dream," said Lucas, closing his eyes. "I dream of clouds of soft, silky satin hanging from the ceiling, feathers floating over the floor, patterns and prints, spots and dots, frills and fancies."

"Dream?" sniffed Shelby. "Sounds like a nightmare!"

"Leave everything to me, Mr. Rumble," said Lucas as he pushed Rumble and Shelby out the door. "Come back tomorrow, and you'll find a palace fit for a king."

"A hotel," said Rumble. "I only want a hotel."

"It's all the same to me," said Lucas.

"Come on," said Shelby. "Let's go!"

"What? And leave him on his own?" asked Rumble.

"Definitely!" said Shelby. "I hate D.I.Y.!"

"D.I.Y.?" asked Rumble, confused.

"Do-It-Yourself," explained Shelby. "It's lots of banging, scraping, gluing, and dripping. Let's get out of here!"

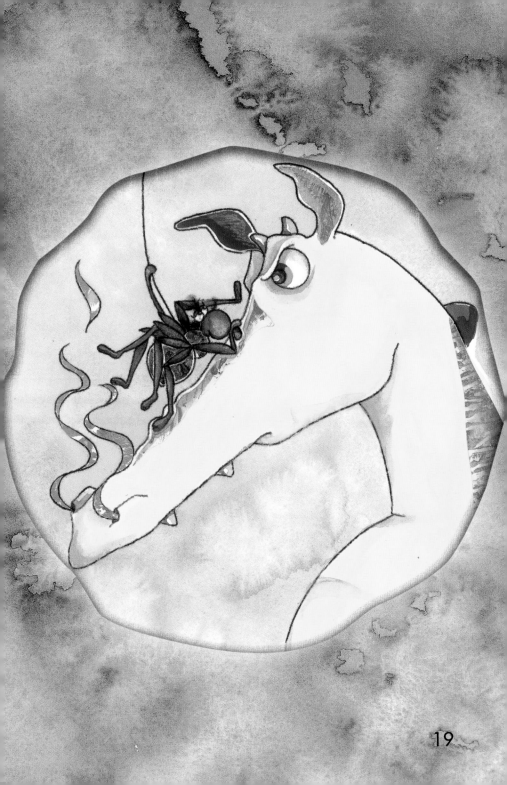

Rumble and Shelby Spider sat on the hillside overlooking the valley.

"I'm not sure," sighed Rumble.

"Not sure about what?" asked Shelby.

"I'm not sure about Lucas Lizard," said Rumble, "or his dreams."

"Well, it's too late now," said Shelby.

Just then, Rumble heard loud bangs and crashes coming from the cave.

"What's that noise?" asked Rumble.

"Don't listen!" said Shelby. "He's knocking down the cave."

"What's that cloud of dust?" asked Rumble.

"Don't look!" said Shelby Spider. "You'll only worry."

"Sorry about the holes!" called Lucas Lizard from the cave. "Sorry about the noise and the dust! My apologies for the mess!"

"Oh, dear," said Rumble. "Oh, dear! Oh, dear!"

Rumble and Shelby Spider sat on the hillside all day. Rumble didn't dare look. He didn't dare listen.

"Hi!" said Buddy Beaver. "That designer's changing your cave. I didn't know you liked purple and yellow spots, Mr. Rumble."

"Oh, dear," said Rumble. "Oh, dear! Oh, dear!"

"Hello!" slurped Todd Toad, the plumber. "I've been talking to your designer. Those flashing green lights will brighten up the lobby, Mr. Rumble."

"Oh, dear," said Rumble. "Oh, dear! Oh, dear!"

That night, Rumble didn't sleep a wink.
The next morning, his eyes were red
and sore from not sleeping.

"You look dreadful," said Shelby Spider.
"Don't worry—it's only a cave!"

"It's a hotel!" sobbed Rumble. "MY hotel!"

"Well, it's ready now," said Shelby. "I think
you should go and look."

Rumble stood on the doorstep of his hotel with his hands over his eyes. He wasn't brave enough to look.

"Open your eyes, Mr. Rumble," said Lucas Lizard. "You won't recognize it!"

"Oh, dear," said Rumble. "Oh, dear! Oh, dear!"

"We were only teasing," said Buddy Beaver and Todd Toad. "You really should look."

Slowly, Rumble moved one hand and then the other. He looked around his new hotel.

"It's beautiful!" he cried as tears rushed to his eyes.

"Of course it's beautiful!" said Lucas Lizard. "I'm a beautiful designer," he added, looking at himself in the mirror.

"I told you I could make this cave into a hotel," Rumble said to Shelby.

"It's a start," said Shelby.

More *Read-it!* Readers

Bright pictures and fun stories help you practice your reading skills. Look for more books at your level.

Alex and Sarah 1-4048-1352-7
Alex and the Team Jersey 1-4048-1024-2
Alex and Toolie 1-4048-1027-7
Clever Cat 1-4048-0560-5
Felicio's Incredible Invention 1-4048-1030-7
Flora McQuack 1-4048-0561-3
Izzie's Idea 1-4048-0644-X
Joe's Day at Rumble's Cave Hotel 1-4048-1339-X
Naughty Nancy 1-4048-0558-3
Parents Do the Weirdest Things! 1-4048-1031-5
The Princess and the Frog 1-4048-0562-1
The Princess and the Tower 1-4048-1184-2
Rumble Meets Harry Hippo 1-4048-1338-1
Rumble Meets Randy Rabbit 1-4048-1337-3
Rumble Meets Shelby Spider 1-4048-1286-5
Rumble Meets Todd Toad 1-4048-1340-3
Rumble Meets Vikki Viper 1-4048-1342-X
Rumble the Dragon's Cave 1-4048-1353-5
Rumble's Famous Granny 1-4048-1336-5
The Truth About Hansel and Gretel 1-4048-0559-1
Willie the Whale 1-4048-0557-5

Looking for a specific title or level? A complete list of *Read-it!* Readers is available on our Web site:
www.picturewindowbooks.com